DO BUNNIES TALK?

DO BUNNIES TALK?

by Dayle Ann Dodds
pictures by A. Dubanevich

HarperCollins*Publishers*

Do Bunnies Talk?
Text copyright © 1992 by Dayle Ann Dodds
Illustrations copyright © 1992 by Arlene Dubanevich
Printed in the U.S.A. All rights reserved.
1 2 3 4 5 6 7 8 9 10
First Edition

Library of Congress Cataloging-in-Publication Data
Dodds, Dayle Ann.
  Do bunnies talk? / by Dayle Ann Dodds ; illustrated by A.
Dubanevich.
      p.   cm.
  Summary: Introduces sounds made by animals, humans, and machines
and the words used to describe those sounds.
  ISBN 0-06-020248-3. — ISBN 0-06-020249-1 (lib. bdg.)
  1. English language—Onomatopoeic words—Juvenile literature.
2. Sounds, Words for—Juvenile literature.   [1. Sounds, Words for.
2. English language—Onomatopoeic words.]   I. Dubanevich, Arlene,
ill.   II. Title.
PE1597.D64   1992   91-13434
428.1—dc20   CIP
                                                        AC

For my parents, with love

—D.D.

For Shelly—not quiet, but a little mysterious

—A.D.

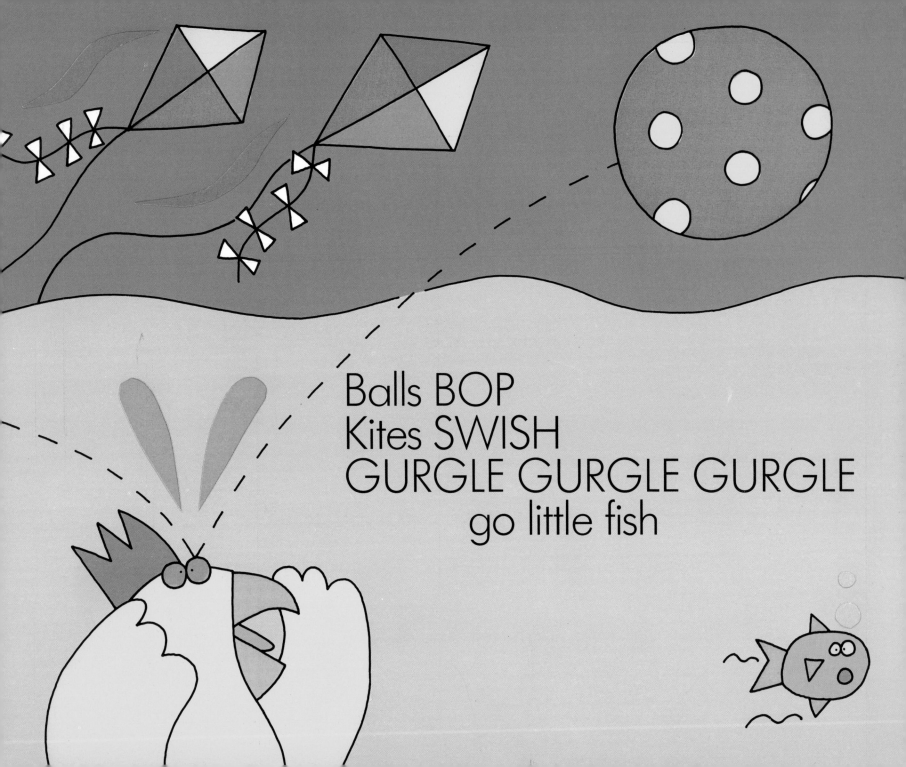

Balls BOP
Kites SWISH
GURGLE GURGLE GURGLE
go little fish

Ducks QUACK
Parrots SQUAWK

But quiet little bunnies never talk

Sheep BAAA
Trucks VA-ROOM
Big bass drums
    go BOOM BOOM BOOM

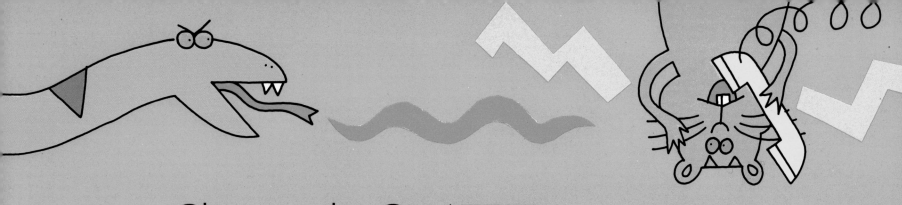

Chipmunks CHATTER
Snakes HISS
Lips SMACK
when they give you a kiss

Bees BUZZZZZZ
Cows MOO

But quiet little bunnies
never do

Clocks TICK-TOCK
Trains TOOT
Mud goes SLISH-SLOSH
under a boot

Cymbals CLASH!
Hens CACKLE

Logs on the fire
CRACKLE
CRACKLE
CRACKLE

Bulls SNORT
Balloons POP

But quiet little bunnies
just hop and hop

Horses NEIGH
Pigs OINK
Pogo sticks go
BOINK
BOINK
BOINK

Rain PITTER-PATTERS
Bubbles FIZZLE
Frying bacon goes
SIZZLE
SIZZLE
SIZZLE

Birds TWITTER
Sticks SNAP
Dancing shoes
TAPPITY-TAP

Roosters COCK-A-DOODLE
Chicks CHEEP-CHEEP

But quiet little bunnies
don't make a peep

Pots CLANG
Glasses CLINK
Drippy faucets
  PLINK PLINK PLINK

Doors C-R-E-A-K
Ghosts go BOO!
Tickly sneezes say
     AH-AH-CHOO!

Donkeys HEE-HAW
Friends say HELLO
Pirates with treasure sing
YO-HO-HO

Hummers HUMMMMMMM
Zippers ZIP
Scissors in your hair
SNIP SNIP SNIP

Cats PURR
Mice SQUEAK

But quiet little bunnies never speak

Geese HONK HONK
Bears GROWL
Wolves in the moonlight
HOWL and HOWL

Cameras CLICK
Fingers SNAP
Thunder and lightning go
CLAP! CLAP!

Teapots WHISTLE
Phones RING-A-LING

But quiet little bunnies NEVER EVER say a thing